DELICIOUS DISNEY
Just for Kids

DELICIOUS DISNEY
Just for Kids

The Disney Chefs
with Pam Brandon

DISNEY
EDITIONS
NEW YORK

INTRODUCTION

WHILE MOST DISNEY FANS ARE KIDS AT HEART, this kid-friendly cookbook is aimed at inspiring young epicures to play in the kitchen. And while there are children's cookbooks that show how to make the simplest of dishes, this book features scrumptious recipes from *Walt Disney World* Resort, *Disneyland* Resort, and the *Disney Cruise Line* ships that are easy enough for kids to create with a little adult supervision. (Though we know some adults will think this book is just perfect for their culinary skills, too.)

Our aim is to make it easy to whip up a delicious treat from a favorite Disney vacation. With some of the recipes, a grown-up needs to be present for chopping with sharp knives, or turning on the stove, but many of these uncomplicated dishes allow kids to work independently and to be introduced to the joy of cooking—and practice math as they measure. Or make it a family activity and let everyone pitch in preparing yummy dishes. Just don't mind the mess.

We hope you are hungry—and ready for some fun!

—Pam Brandon

OPPOSITE: *Author Pam Brandon and Walt Disney World Food & Beverage Marketing Manager Karen Haynes pose with Chef Mickey.*

TABLE OF CONTENTS

Bircher Muesli

✳ DISNEY CRUISE LINE SERVICES

SERVES 6

1. Combine oats, orange juice, milk, honey, yogurt, vanilla extract, and raisins in a large bowl. Stir to combine and make "muesli."

2. Cover bowl with plastic wrap. Refrigerate overnight.

3. In the morning, stir almonds or walnuts into mix. Add grated apple, if using.

4. Whip cream in a medium-sized bowl until stiff peaks form. Fold whipped cream into muesli. Add more milk to reach desired consistency. Sprinkle with cinnamon or nutmeg, if desired, and serve with fresh fruit of your choice.

CHEF MICKEY SAYS: Muesli is the German word for "mixture," a popular breakfast cereal in Europe.

3 cups old-fashioned oats
(not quick oats)

¾ cup fresh orange juice

1 ⅓ cups low-fat milk or soy milk

⅓ cup honey

½ cup vanilla yogurt

½ teaspoon vanilla extract

¼ cup raisins

2 tablespoons chopped almonds
or walnuts

1 green apple, peeled and coarsely grated, optional

½ cup light cream, chilled

Ground nutmeg or cinnamon,
to taste, optional

1 to 2 cups mixed fresh fruit
(such as raspberries, strawberries, melon, apple, banana, grapes, kiwi, pineapple, or mango)

Chocolate, Peanut Butter, and Banana French Toast

DISNEY'S PCH GRILL ✻ DISNEY'S PARADISE PIER HOTEL ✻ DISNEYLAND RESORT

SERVES 4

8 thick slices day-old challah bread

2 ripe bananas

¼ cup chocolate chips

½ cup creamy peanut butter

6 eggs, lightly beaten

¾ cup low-fat chocolate milk

1 teaspoon ground cinnamon

¼ teaspoon salt

Chocolate syrup and powdered sugar, optional

1. Preheat oven to 350°F. Coat a 13x9x2-inch baking pan with nonstick spray. Set aside.

2. Cut bread into 1-inch cubes and place in a large bowl. Slice bananas into ¼-inch slices, and add to bowl. Stir in chocolate chips.

3. Combine peanut butter, eggs, chocolate milk, cinnamon, and salt in a blender. Process until smooth.

4. Pour egg mixture over bread mixture. Stir gently until bread cubes have absorbed egg mixture.

5. Pour mixture into prepared baking pan. Bake for 35 to 40 minutes, or until top is golden brown.

6. Before serving, drizzle with chocolate syrup and dust with powdered sugar, if desired.

CHEF MICKEY SAYS: Made with eggs and honey, challah is traditional Jewish yeast bread that makes the best French toast.

African Fruit Fool

SERVES 6

1. Combine pineapple, apple, mango, papaya, grapes, bananas, and coconut in a large bowl. Gently stir to combine. Stir in sweetened condensed milk.

2. Whip cream until soft peaks form. Add vanilla and continue to beat just until stiff peaks form. Working in batches, gently fold whipped cream into fruit mixture.

3. Cover bowl with plastic wrap. Refrigerate until cold, approximately 30 minutes.

CHEF MICKEY SAYS: To cube a mango, use a paring knife to cut off a "cheek" (roundish side). Start by gently making parallel cuts down to the skin, but do not cut through the skin. Repeat the process going the other direction until you have a "grid." Put down the knife, pick up the mango, and with two hands push up on the skin underneath to invert the mango. Slide the knife along the skin to free the cubes.

1 cup diced fresh pineapple

1 green apple, peeled and diced

1 small, ripe mango, peeled and diced (about 1 cup)

1 cup diced fresh papaya

2 cups red seedless grapes

3 bananas, peeled and sliced

1 cup shredded coconut

¾ cup sweetened condensed milk

1 cup cream, chilled

1 teaspoon vanilla extract

Saratoga Springs House Salad

THE ARTIST'S PALETTE ❈ DISNEY'S SARATOGA SPRINGS RESORT & SPA ❈ WALT DISNEY WORLD RESORT

4 cups baby greens

¼ cup plus 2 tablespoons
Poppy Seed Dressing
(recipe follows), divided

2 tablespoons dried cranberries

2 tablespoons dried blueberries

2 tablespoons chopped almonds
or walnuts

½ red apple, cored and diced

POPPY SEED DRESSING

¼ cup sugar

¼ cup fresh lemon juice

1 teaspoon diced
or granulated onion

½ teaspoon Dijon mustard

¼ teaspoon coarse salt

⅓ cup canola oil

½ tablespoon poppy seeds

SERVES 4

1. Place greens in large bowl. Add dressing, and lightly toss to combine.

2. Divide dressed greens among 4 serving plates. Top each serving with ½ tablespoon dried cranberries, ½ tablespoon dried blueberries, ½ tablespoon almonds or walnuts, and ¼ of the diced apple. Evenly drizzle with remaining dressing, if desired. Serve immediately.

Poppy Seed Dressing

1. Place sugar, lemon juice, onion, Dijon, and salt in a blender. Process until smooth.

2. With the blender running, slowly drizzle oil through the lid. Process until dressing comes together. Add poppy seed and pulse to combine.

CHEF MICKEY SAYS: When you toss a salad, add anything you like—dried fruits, nuts, cheese, fresh fruit, chopped turkey, or ham. Be creative!

Cheeseburger Calzones

MAKES 8 (7-INCH) CALZONES

For meatballs:

1. Preheat oven to 325°F. Line a 13x9x2-inch baking pan with aluminum foil.

2. Combine all ingredients in a large bowl and knead until thoroughly mixed. Form mixture into 12 (2-inch) meatballs.

3. Place meatballs in prepared pan and bake for 25 to 30 minutes, or until cooked through.

For calzones:

1. Preheat oven to 350°F.

2. Divide dough into 12 equal portions. Roll out each portion into a 5-inch circle.

3. For each calzone, cut one slice of cheese in half diagonally and place one triangle of cheese on the lower half of a dough circle. Chop one meatball into bite-sized pieces and place on top of cheese triangle. Top with remaining cheese triangle. Fold top portion of dough over filling and crimp edges to seal.

4. Place calzones on baking sheets and bake for 15 to 20 minutes, or until lightly browned.

5. While calzones are baking, warm sauce in a saucepan over medium-low heat.

6. To serve, pour ¼ cup of pasta or pizza sauce over each calzone, or serve sauce on the side, if desired.

CHEF MICKEY SAYS: Use a kitchen timer to help you remember when to take the calzones out of the oven.

MEATBALLS

12 ounces ground beef

½ cup Italian-style bread crumbs

¼ cup chopped onion

2 eggs

½ cup water

2 tablespoons grated Romano cheese

1 teaspoon garlic powder

CALZONES

2 ½ pounds pre-made pizza dough

12 slices American or cheddar cheese

1 (24-ounce) jar pasta or pizza sauce

Macaroni & Cheese

JIKO—THE COOKING PLACE ❊ *DISNEY'S ANIMAL KINGDOM* LODGE ❊ *WALT DISNEY WORLD* RESORT

SERVES 4 TO 6

- 3 tablespoons unsalted butter
- 3 tablespoons all-purpose flour
- 2 ½ cups whole milk (can substitute 2 percent milk)
- 8 ounces shredded Italian cheese blend (such as mozzarella, Asiago, fontina, and provolone)
- ¼ teaspoon coarse salt
- ¼ teaspoon ground black pepper
- 1 pound elbow macaroni, cooked and kept warm

1. Melt butter in a medium saucepan over medium heat. Add flour, stirring until combined. Cook, stirring frequently, for 5 minutes, or until golden (do not let brown).

2. Add milk to butter mixture, whisking until completely smooth and no lumps remain.

3. Simmer mixture, stirring frequently, until sauce coats the back of a spoon, 5 to 8 minutes.

4. Add cheese to saucepan in batches, stirring until completely melted. Add salt and pepper, stirring to combine.

5. Place cooked macaroni in a large bowl. Add cheese sauce, stirring to combine. Serve immediately.

CHEF MICKEY SAYS: Asiago and fontina are Italian cheeses that add a rich, nutty flavor to this mac 'n' cheese.

Lemon Soda Float

CARNATION CAFE ✳ DISNEYLAND PARK ✳ DISNEYLAND RESORT

SERVES 4

1. Divide ice cream among 4 glasses. Pour 2 cups lemon soda over ice cream in each glass.

2. Top with whipped cream and a cherry, if desired.

1 pint vanilla ice cream

1 (2-liter) bottle lemon-lime soda

Whipped cream, maraschino cherries, for garnish, optional

Chicken Caesar Wrap

❋ DISNEY CRUISE LINE SERVICES

SERVES 4

1. Lightly sprinkle chicken tenders with paprika, salt, and pepper. Sear chicken in a large sauté pan over medium heat until golden brown and cooked through, about 4 minutes per side. Set aside to cool. Refrigerate until cold.

2. Cut chicken into bite-sized pieces. Combine chopped chicken, chopped romaine, and ¼ cup Caesar dressing in a large bowl. Toss to combine. Add additional dressing, if desired.

3. Lay spinach tortillas on a work surface. Spread a thin layer of remaining Caesar dressing on each tortilla. Evenly divide Caesar salad mix among centers of spinach tortillas. Roll tortilla up around filling. Cut each roll in half diagonally. Serve immediately.

CHEF MICKEY SAYS: Tortillas come in lots of flavors, from spinach to tomato to roasted red pepper. But a plain one will work just fine.

½ pound chicken tenders

½ teaspoon paprika

¼ teaspoon coarse salt

¼ teaspoon ground black pepper

2 hearts or 1 small head romaine lettuce, cut into bite-sized pieces

½ cup favorite Caesar dressing

4 medium spinach tortillas, warmed

BLT Tomato Soup

SCI-FI DINE-IN THEATER RESTAURANT ❋ *DISNEY'S HOLLYWOOD STUDIOS* ❋ *WALT DISNEY WORLD* RESORT

SERVES 6 TO 8

- 8 slices bacon
- 2 tablespoons butter
- 1 teaspoon chopped garlic
- 3 tablespoons chopped onion
- 1 tablespoon finely diced carrots
- 2 tablespoons flour
- 4 cups chicken stock or broth
- 1 (28-ounce) can crushed tomatoes
- 1 teaspoon tomato paste
- Coarse salt, freshly ground black pepper, to taste
- 1 cup cream
- 6 to 8 thin baguette slices
- 2 tablespoons olive oil
- 2 teaspoons Italian seasoning
- 12 fresh basil leaves, chopped; ½ cup shredded lettuce; 8 tablespoons diced fresh tomatoes; chopped bacon, for garnish

1. Cook bacon in a large skillet over medium heat. Remove from pan, drain on paper towels, coarsely chop, and reserve for garnish. Reserve drippings.

2. Melt butter and stir in bacon drippings in a medium-sized saucepan over medium heat. Add garlic, onion, and carrots, and cook until onion is transparent, about 5 minutes. Stir in flour.

3. Add chicken stock or broth, crushed tomatoes, and tomato paste, blending all ingredients. Season with salt and pepper, and cook over medium heat for 30 minutes.

4. Remove from stove; puree in blender and return to pan. Add cream and simmer. Season with salt and pepper, to taste.

5. To make croutons, drizzle baguette slices with olive oil, sprinkle with Italian dressing, and bake at 350°F for 5 to 6 minutes or until golden brown. Remove from oven.

6. Ladle soup into bowls. Top with croutons and add other garnishes, as desired.

CHEF MICKEY SAYS: For a recipe with lots of ingredients, read the recipe from start to finish, and be sure you have all the ingredients and equipment assembled before you start. You can even measure and chop before you start cooking.

Double-stuffed Broccoli-and-Cheese Baked Potatoes

TROUBADOUR TAVERN ❖ DISNEYLAND PARK ❖ DISNEYLAND RESORT

SERVES 4

1. Preheat oven to 400°F.

2. Place potatoes on a baking sheet. Prick each potato with a fork. Bake for 1 hour. Set aside to cool to room temperature.

3. Slice the top quarter lengthwise off each baked potato. Carefully scoop out insides, leaving ¼ inch of potato on the skin.

4. Combine potato and milk in a large bowl, and mash. Stir in cheese, sour cream, broccoli, bacon, green onions, and salt.

5. Spoon mixture back into shells, and place on baking sheet. Evenly top potatoes with remaining cheese. Cover lightly with foil. Bake for 20 minutes. Remove foil, and bake 8 minutes more, or until cheese is melted and bubbly. Set aside to cool for 3 minutes before serving.

CHEF MICKEY SAYS: Always have an adult help you take things out of the oven—and use pot holders. The inside of the oven door and racks are hot, so don't touch!

4 large russet potatoes, about ¾ pound each

½ cup whole or 2 percent milk

1 ¼ cups shredded cheddar cheese, divided

1 ¼ cups sour cream

1 cup diced steamed broccoli

5 slices bacon, cooked and crumbled

4 green onions, thinly sliced

1 teaspoon coarse salt

Ginger Green Beans

SERVES 4

1 tablespoon vegetable oil

1 tablespoon minced ginger

½ pound green beans, cut into
1-inch pieces

Coarse salt, to taste

1. Heat oil in a sauté pan over medium heat. Add ginger and cook for
    30 seconds, stirring constantly.

2. Add green beans. Cook, tossing frequently, 5 to 6 minutes, or until crisp-
    tender. Sprinkle lightly with salt to taste. Serve immediately.

CHEF MICKEY SAYS: Ginger is a plant from tropical and subtropical regions.
We use the bumpy root that has a peppery and slightly sweet taste and a
spicy fragrance.

Baby Carrots in Orange Glaze

CHEF MICKEY'S ✳ *DISNEY'S CONTEMPORARY RESORT* ✳ *WALT DISNEY WORLD RESORT*

SERVES 4

1. Place carrots in large sauté pan with a tight-fitting lid over medium-high heat. Add ¼ cup water. Steam until carrots are crisp-tender, about 4 minutes. Drain any excess water.

2. Lower heat to medium. Add butter to carrots, stirring to coat. Add brown sugar, orange juice, marmalade, and salt to the pan, stirring to combine.

3. Simmer, stirring, until glaze thickens slightly and carrots are tender, 5 to 6 minutes. Serve immediately.

CHEF MICKEY SAYS: Always wash and dry vegetables before you use them.

1 pound baby carrots
4 tablespoons butter
1 tablespoon brown sugar
¼ cup orange juice
2 tablespoons orange marmalade
½ teaspoon salt

Ratatouille

CRYSTAL PALACE ❋ MAGIC KINGDOM PARK ❋ WALT DISNEY WORLD RESORT

SERVES 4

2 tablespoons olive oil

½ large red bell pepper, seeded and diced

½ small red onion, diced

1 teaspoon chopped garlic (about 1 large clove)

1 medium or 2 small zucchini, diced

1 small yellow squash, diced

1 cup diced eggplant (about ½ medium eggplant)

¾ teaspoon coarse salt

¼ teaspoon black pepper

1 teaspoon fresh thyme leaves

1 cup canned tomato puree

½ cup water

2 tablespoons chopped fresh basil

1. Heat oil in a large sauté pan over medium heat. Add bell pepper, onion, and garlic. Cook, stirring often, until tender, about 5 minutes. Add zucchini, squash, eggplant, salt, pepper, and thyme. Cook, stirring often, until vegetables are tender, about 5 minutes.

2. Add tomato puree and water. Cover pan, and reduce heat to low. Simmer until vegetables are very tender, about 25 minutes. Add basil, and stir to combine. Serve immediately or at room temperature.

CHEF MICKEY SAYS: Besides being the name of a blockbuster Disney•Pixar animated film, ratatouille is a delicious big bowl of veggies simmered in olive oil that is a popular dish in the French region of Provence. It's delicious served hot or room temperature.

Kids' Flatbread

SANAA RESTAURANT ❊ *DISNEY'S ANIMAL KINGDOM* VILLAS – KIDANI VILLAGE ❊ *WALT DISNEY WORLD* RESORT

SERVES 4

4 (4-ounce) naan (Indian flatbreads; may substitute pita bread)

¾ cup prepared pizza sauce

2 cups shredded low-fat mozzarella cheese

1. Preheat oven to 350°.
2. Spread 3 tablespoons pizza sauce over each naan bread. Sprinkle each with ½ cup cheese.
3. Bake for 10 to 12 minutes, or until cheese is melted and bubbly. Cool for 3 minutes before cutting and serving.

CHEF MICKEY SAYS: Naan bread is an East Indian, white-flour flatbread, traditionally baked in a tandoor oven. The flattened round of dough bakes in less than 60 seconds on the side of the high-heat oven. It makes a quick, thin pizza crust.

Big Thunder Ribs

BIG THUNDER RANCH BARBECUE ❊ *DISNEYLAND* PARK ❊ *DISNEYLAND* RESORT

SERVES 4 TO 6

1. Sprinkle Citrus BBQ Rub on both sides of ribs, rubbing the meat to adhere. Cover with plastic wrap. Refrigerate for 8 hours, or overnight.

2. Preheat oven to 350°F. Place ribs in a roasting pan or on a baking sheet, and pour water into pan. Cover with foil and roast for 1 hour.

3. Remove the pan from oven and uncover. Pour off any excess water. Evenly coat top of ribs with barbecue sauce. Return pan to oven and roast for 30 minutes more.

4. Remove the pan from the oven and cover lightly with foil. Let ribs rest for 10 minutes.

5. Slice the ribs between each bone with a serrated knife. Serve immediately.

1 ½ cups Citrus Roundup BBQ Rub
1 (4-pound) rack pork spareribs, trimmed of excess fat
½ cup water
1 cup favorite barbecue sauce

Citrus Roundup BBQ Rub

Combine all ingredients in a medium bowl. Stir to combine.

CHEF MICKEY SAYS: "BBQ Rub" is a mixture of finely ground dry seasonings that add extra flavor to the ribs. Depending how much you use it can also form a nice crust on the meat.

CITRUS ROUNDUP BBQ RUB
2 ½ tablespoons lemon pepper
2 tablespoons seasoning salt
2 tablespoons paprika
1 tablespoon sugar
1 tablespoon brown sugar
1 tablespoon ground cumin
1 tablespoon chili powder
1 tablespoon garlic powder
1 tablespoon onion powder
¼ tablespoon cayenne pepper

Potato Gnocchi

✳ *Disney Cruise Line Services*

3 pounds russet potatoes

2 cups all-purpose flour

Pinch of coarse salt,
freshly ground black pepper

Pinch of nutmeg

1 extra large egg

1 (24-ounce) jar of favorite pasta
or pesto sauce

Fresh Parmesan cheese
for garnish, optional

SERVES 6

1. In a large pot over high heat, boil the potatoes whole until soft, about 45 minutes. Allow to cool somewhat, but not completely.

2. Peel and halve warm potatoes; pass through a potato ricer onto a lightly floured work surface. Potatoes should not be hot—if they are, they will cook the egg.

3. In a mixing bowl, whisk together flour, salt, pepper, and nutmeg. Sprinkle over the potatoes.

4. Make a well in the center of the potatoes and add the egg. Stir with a fork to incorporate the egg, and then knead by hand until dough is uniform, about 5 minutes.

5. Set a large pot of water over high heat to boil. Divide the dough into eight equal portions. Using the palms of your hands, roll each portion into a rope, roughly ¾-inch in diameter. Cut each rope into 1-inch pieces.

6. Roll each piece horizontally between your index finger and the tines of a fork. (Gnocchi can be cooked immediately following step 5, but the ridges are traditional.)

7. Pour pasta sauce into a large saucepan over low heat.

8. In small batches, drop gnocchi into boiling water. Cook until they rise to the surface, about 1 minute. Use a slotted spoon to remove gnocchi and add them to the pasta sauce. Once all the gnocchi have been cooked, serve immediately.

CHEF MICKEY SAYS: Gnocchi (NYOH-kee) is Italian for "dumplings," and most gnocchi is made from potatoes. It's delicious with red sauce, but you can also try a pesto sauce, made with fresh basil, garlic, nuts, Parmesan cheese, and olive oil. Or just lightly coat gnocchi with butter and fresh Parmesan cheese.

Moist Apple Cake

✳ *DISNEY CRUISE LINE SERVICES*

SERVES 8 TO 12

1. Preheat oven to 350°F. Spray bottom and sides of a 9-inch springform pan with nonstick spray.

2. Sift flour, baking soda, nutmeg, cinnamon, and salt into a large bowl. Set aside.

3. Combine brown sugar and oil in the bowl of an electric mixer fitted with the whisk attachment. Beat on medium speed to combine. Add eggs. Beat at medium speed for 5 minutes. With a spoon or rubber spatula, stir in diced apple.

4. Fold flour mixture into batter. Pour the mixture into prepared pan.

5. Bake for 45 to 50 minutes, or until the cake springs back when touched.

6. Dust with powdered sugar or serve with freshly whipped cream, if desired.

CHEF MICKEY SAYS: A springform pan is a two-piece pan that has sides that can be removed. This makes it easier to take the cake out of the pan.

1 ¾ cups all-purpose flour

1 teaspoon baking soda

⅛ teaspoon ground nutmeg

⅛ teaspoon ground cinnamon

Pinch of salt

1 ⅓ cups brown sugar

1 cup extra virgin olive oil

2 eggs

3 Granny Smith apples, peeled, cored, and diced

Fresh whipped cream or powdered sugar, optional

Florentine Cookies

BIERGARTEN RESTAURANT ❋ GERMANY PAVILION, *EPCOT®* ❋ *WALT DISNEY WORLD* RESORT

MAKES 32 (2x3-INCH) COOKIES

1. Preheat oven to 350°F.

2. Cut a sheet of parchment paper to fit inside a regular sheet pan. Place the parchment paper rectangle on the counter, and place cookie dough on the parchment paper.

3. Roll out cookie dough to cover most of the rectangle, leaving a ½-inch border of paper. The dough should be approximately ⅛-inch thick.

4. Carefully transfer dough on parchment to the sheet pan. Spoon jam onto dough, and use the back of a spoon to spread it evenly over dough. Evenly sprinkle with almonds and sugar.

5. Bake for 15 to 18 minutes. Transfer sheet pan to a wire rack to cool completely, at least 1 hour. When cool, slide baked dough off of sheet pan. Cut into rectangles using a pizza cutter or a knife.

6. Store cookies in an airtight container, separating layers with pieces of parchment paper to prevent them from sticking together.

CHEF MICKEY SAYS: If you don't like raspberry jam, you can use your favorite flavor.

1 (16.5-ounce) package refrigerated sugar cookie dough
1 cup raspberry jam
½ cup sliced almonds
½ tablespoon granulated sugar

Island Navigator

❉ DISNEY CRUISE LINE SERVICES

SERVES 2

1 cup pineapple juice

⅓ cup coconut cream

6 to 8 ice cubes

1 cup vanilla ice cream or frozen vanilla yogurt

Pineapple triangles, for garnish

1. Combine pineapple juice and coconut cream in a blender. Blend to combine.

2. Add ice, and pulse until ice is crushed. Add ice cream, and blend until smooth.

3. Garnish with pineapple triangles, if desired. Serve immediately.

No-Bake Granola Treats

DISNEY'S CONTEMPORARY RESORT BAKERY ✳ *WALT DISNEY WORLD RESORT*

MAKES 12 (2x2-INCH) TREATS

1. In a medium saucepan over low heat, melt marshmallows and butter. Add peanut butter, stirring to combine. Remove from heat. Stir in granola.

2. Spoon mixture into a 6x8-inch baking dish. Lightly press mixture into pan using lightly moistened hands. Sprinkle top of mixture with chocolate chips, lightly pressing the chocolate chips into mixture.

3. Set aside at room temperature to cool for 30 minutes. Cut into 12 pieces. Store treats in an airtight container at room temperature for up to 1 week.

3 ½ cups miniature marshmallows

2 tablespoons unsalted butter

3 tablespoons smooth peanut butter

1 ½ cups granola

¼ cup miniature semisweet chocolate chips

ACKNOWLEDGMENTS

A million thanks to the wonderful team who helped create this book. To Karen Haynes for staying upbeat and keeping us on track. To Katie Farmand for beautiful food styling and for patiently testing and retesting recipes. To gifted photographer Gary Bogdon and his assistant Jeremy Kyle Bryan. To our adorable kid models: Marlie Bogdon, Jackson Hogan, Jacob Hogan, Kathryn McCoy, Ariel Nicole McMillan, Ethan Pouncey, Jordan Pouncey, Ayden Pouncey, and Brittain Rainville. To Betsy Singer in Disney Merchandise who gave us the green light. To Karlos Siquieros and Christopher Maggetti for rounding up *Disneyland* recipes, and to Christine Weissman at *Disney Cruise Line* Services. To our talented New York team, editor Jessie Ward (also an extraordinary recipe tester), designer Jon Glick, and editorial director Wendy Lefkon.

For information address Disney Editions, 114 Fifth Avenue, New York, NY 10011-5690.
Printed in Singapore
First Edition
10 9 8 7 6 5 4 3 2 1
Reinforced binding
Library of Congress Cataloging-in-Publication Data on file.
ISBN 978-1-4231-1993-7
F850-6835-5-11001

The Official Community for Disney Fans
Disney.com/D23